I0621982

A Candied Christmas

Candied Crush #29

Charity Parkerson

Punk & Sissy Publications

Copyright

—Warning: This book is intended for readers over the age of 18. Some of my books contain allusions to past abuse and trauma. I try to never have anything triggering on page and treat every situation with care.

Editor: BZ Hercules & Consultants

Contents

Introduction   1

Chapter One   3

Chapter Two   15

Chapter Three   37

Chapter Four   70

Chapter Five   82

Chapter Six   108

About the Author   114

Introduction

ROSCOE AND REMINGTON HAVE spent their entire marriage as an open couple. Now they've met their third. They're done playing.

Everyone in certain circles knows Remington and Roscoe for the players they are. It's equally well known that nothing can break them. They've been together their whole lives and anyone else is merely a night of fun. Until Leo comes to town, that is.

Leo moved to L.A. after signing on to model with a popular fashion guru. Everyone keeps telling him to visit the best coffeehouse around: The Back Porch. No one warned him about Roscoe and Remington.

With the holidays around the corner, Leo needs a distraction. The naughty married couple seems as good of a choice as any. The last thing he expects is the immediate connection... or their determination. But can the pair win him?

A Candied Christmas is a short addition to Charity Parkerson's Candied Crush series. Read along to find love during the holidays.

Chapter One

THE BACK PORCH LOOKED like someone's oversized house on the outside. That was Leo's first thought as he headed for the door. One of his model friends had been suggesting the coffeehouse since Leo came to L.A., but Leo hadn't found the time to come before now. Leo stood in the parking lot and took several breaths before heading for the door. All his life, Leo had suffered from anxiety. He did everything his therapist told him, plus he used some of Mom's advice to get through every new adventure. Leo held his head high, stiffened his spine, pretended he was on the catwalk, and opened the door.

The scent of coffee and pastries wafted out. Leo scanned the cafe, looking for an empty table. The Christmas tree in the back corner startled Leo from his act. He had been working so much, he had forgotten all about the holidays. His mind scrambled for the date. Damn. Thanksgiving had been last week, and he had missed it. It was for the best.

"I have an empty table over here."

Leo tore his gaze away from the tree to focus on the man waiting for his attention. He was huge. His dark skin and amber eyes had Leo's attention. Ezra had warned Leo about the owner Wrecker's beauty, but there was no way Leo could have prepared himself for Wrecker's odd-colored stare. It was mesmerizing. Still, by Ezra's description, Leo would have recognized Wrecker anywhere. The man should be modeling. With a smile and a nod, Leo allowed Wrecker to lead him to the empty table he referenced. He sat while Wrecker set a menu in front of him.

Leo pushed it away. "I don't need this. Ezra says I have to try a white geisha and whatever cake you've baked for the day. I can't disobey a direct order."

A bright smile lit Wrecker's features, making him twice as gorgeous. "You're a friend of Ezra?"

Leo nodded. "We've been working on the same fashion show for the past month. This is the first chance I've had to stop by."

"Well, then," Wrecker said, scooping up the menu. "In that case, let this first order be on me. I'd love to see if I can make a regular out of you."

The smile pulling at Leo's lips was genuine for the first time in a while. For that reason alone, he already knew he would be back. "I'm game to let you try."

With a chuckle, Wrecker walked away. Leo glanced around, checking out the place. There was a stage in the back of the building next to the Christmas tree. Ezra had told him they had an open mic night. Just in case Leo had any hidden talents. He did not. Being pretty was literally all he had going for him. Before three months ago, Leo would have also said he had the world's best family. He couldn't say that anymore.

A wave of sadness washed over him. He tried focusing on the coffeehouse patrons to busy his mind. Leo couldn't think about his father's betrayal and what it had cost him. He had to think about something else. There seemed to be a lot of couples sitting huddled together. Leo wondered if this was a hot spot for gay men to take their dates. One pair in particular caught Leo's attention. Not only were they both dark-haired, light-eyed, and strikingly beautiful, but they were also staring intently at Leo.

Leo looked away.

Wrecker appeared at his side. "Here you go. One white geisha and a slice of my famous chocolate cake."

The smell hit him. "Mmm. This looks amazing. Thank you." He hadn't meant anything so much in his life. The cake made his mouth water.

Wrecker winked and walked away. As Leo picked up his fork, he made a mental note to leave Wrecker a huge tip. As he scooped a bite into his mouth, his eyes fell closed. He couldn't recall the last time he had anything sweet. Leo would definitely have to skip dinner tonight and spend an extra hour at the gym in the morning, but it would be worth it. The cake was divine. Leo lost himself in a moment of indulgence. He hadn't allowed himself even the tiniest bit of peace since landing in L.A. Signing with Dame Wylde—the biggest fashion guru in the United States—Leo had to be the letter of perfection. He couldn't let himself slip. People slit throats to be in his shoes. Leo couldn't forget it.

"Hi."

Leo blinked at the sudden appearance of the two men who had been watching him earlier. He forced his thoughts away from his cake. "Hello."

The pair smiled. The closest of the two did all the talking. "I'm Remington." He motioned his friend's way. "This is Roscoe. May we join you?"

"Um." Leo glanced around, unsure of what to do. He swore everyone watched them. "I guess."

The pair sat. They immediately leaned closer to each other. A tide of longing tried to pull Leo under. They were visibly in love. Their body language gave away everything about them. He knew without looking they held hands beneath the table. Surely they only meant to be nice by joining him.

"I'm Leo," Leo said, realizing he hadn't introduced himself yet.

Roscoe had light blue eyes. Remington's were light gray. Both sets flashed with interest. "Leo," they said simultaneously.

Leo blinked. They were a bit much. He thought about rescinding his invitation. Then Roscoe spoke and Leo swore his soul melted.

"We saw you sitting alone and knew we had to remedy that." Lord, his voice was deep and perfect. It was like angels sang.

"I'm new in town, so I don't know many people yet."

They nodded their understanding. Remington seemed to be the lead voice of the two. "Where are you from?"

"Texas. What about you two?"

"Here." They spoke in unison again. That took some getting used to for

Leo. For a reason he couldn't explain, the pair overwhelmed him.

Leo refused to let that get in the way of him making new friends. "Sorry. It seems like everyone I've met since I moved to town is from somewhere else. It's nice to meet locals, though. You must know all the best places."

Roscoe's eyes flashed with humor. "We definitely know how to find hidden gems."

Heat filled Leo's cheeks. He fought the urge to fan his face. While he was used to having men flirt with him, this was different. He had never been approached by a couple. Plus, Leo couldn't decide if they were flirting. It was possible he was the one a little too interested, and they were just being nice. That was crazy, though. He needed to set that bullshit aside. Leo hyper-focused on their relationship, trying to kill his growing interest. He could not let his interest in this pair grow.

Leo had to do everything he could to remind himself the two were obviously dating. "How long have you two been together?" Leo took a bite of his cake while Remington answered.

"All our lives. Our mothers are best friends. They intentionally got pregnant at the same time, so their kids could be best friends."

Roscoe nodded. "I'm three weeks younger, so we had to wait three weeks after Remington turned eighteen so we could get married."

That was it. They were married. He was being ridiculous. Leo had been too long without sex. That was all. He took another bite of his cake.

"What are you doing tonight?"

At Remington's question, Leo froze with the fork halfway to his mouth. His gaze moved between them. Roscoe leaned across the table and ate the bite of cake. As his full lips closed around Leo's fork, Leo's cock stirred. He could picture Roscoe on his knees.

Leo cleared his throat and pushed his plate the pair's way. "You can finish this if you want. Dame will kill me if I gain a single pound and throw off his designs."

Remington pushed the plate back his way. "Go ahead and finish. We'll keep the calories at bay."

Leo's eyebrows rose.

Roscoe pulled a pen from his back pocket and snagged Leo's napkin. He looked at his watch and then drew a tiny map under the address he scribbled. "Come by around seven. That should give you plenty of time to panic, change your mind, and then get over your doubts and change it back." He slid the napkin Leo's way. His sexy gaze never wavered from Leo's. "You won't regret us."

Leo was absolutely sure that was true because he wouldn't be going. The pair stood and walked away. They weren't quick about it. Leo had plenty of time to say he wouldn't be there. He didn't. Leo went back to eating his cake. His gaze moved toward the napkin without thinking. An address, a tiny map, and two phone numbers stared back at him. He wouldn't go, but the offer flattered the fuck out of him. It wasn't a proposition he got every day. The pair was spectacular. He could see himself between them. Leo wouldn't do it, but he could picture it.

Chapter Two

ROSCOE AND REMINGTON HAD grown up glued at the hip. Over the years, they had shared more men than Remington could recall, and Remington was always down to share more. But something had shifted in their relationship over a year ago. A woman about their mothers' age had simply appeared at their table at The Back Porch. She had sat without invitation, and said, "Don't worry. You'll find your third. There's no need to search so hard."

Roscoe had squeezed Remington's hand beneath the table and something unnamed passed between—like a silent truce. They stopped hunting that day.

Fifteen months had passed without a single extra person between them. They didn't discuss it. They simply stopped, as if they needed to reassess their life together. They were happy being only a pair. There really wasn't anything missing from them. Remington couldn't explain their constant search for another. Until he knew why they did what they did, they needed to stop.

Ultimately, they had always only wanted each other. Everyone else was just fun. Their love couldn't be touched. They would grow old and die together, no matter what. That was never in question. They couldn't be broken. Remington thought it was possible they would touch no one else again. Then Leo had swept through the door.

Roscoe had immediately leaned closer. Remington's breath had caught. They hadn't discussed what they would do. As one, they had simply stood and moved to join Leo. Since they had gotten home, they still hadn't talked about the encounter. Every few minutes, they met each other's gaze and smiled. Remington felt Roscoe's growing anticipation. He didn't doubt Roscoe felt his too.

At ten minutes after seven, Remington deflated a hair. Roscoe climbed into his lap on the couch. "It doesn't look like Leo's coming."

Remington pulled Roscoe in for a kiss. Their lips clung. Love washed over Remington. "Do you want to talk about it?"

Roscoe pressed his forehead to Remington's. They stared into each other's eyes. He swore sometimes they could read each other's mind. "There was something about him."

There was. Remington couldn't explain it. "I know."

When Leo had swept into the coffeehouse, his platinum hair had caught the light and their attention. When they had joined him at his table, Remington had been blown away by the color of Leo's eyes. They were uniquely green. Almost a sea foam in coloration. Beautiful. Remington had felt a tug in his chest. The three of them would have been gorgeous together. There was more to it than that, though, and Remington couldn't put a voice to it.

A knock landed on the door. They glanced toward it before meeting each other's stare again. Together, they scrambled from the couch and answered. Leo stood on the other side.

"Sorry I'm late. I decided last minute to pick up some wine. Then I couldn't decide whether to get red or white, because I didn't know which you two liked, so I got both."

Roscoe leaned closer into Remington's side and Remington swore he read his husband's mind. Leo had shown. They weren't crazy. There was something about him. That thought wouldn't stop pressing its way into Remington's mind.

As one, they made room for Leo to pass. "We love all forms of alcohol."

"Your thoughtfulness is definitely appreciated," Roscoe said, finishing for Remington.

Remington inhaled as Leo passed. He smelled like honeysuckle.

Leo glanced over his shoulder, no doubt catching Remington and Roscoe staring like lions ready to pounce. He didn't look worried. "Your house is amazing, by the way. I almost turned around when I saw the neighborhood." His eyes swam with laughter. "I've never felt so poor."

Roscoe didn't hold back. "Now is probably a good time to admit that we do porn, in case you want to run."

"Really?" Leo didn't sound horrified. Merely curious.

Remington nodded. "Not like on a movie set where we're directed to fuck whoever is chosen for us. We have an online following. It's only us together or in solo vids."

Leo nodded. "I can imagine you're very popular."

A smile snapped to Remington's lips. Leo seemed calm and accepting. He looked like a babe in the woods. Remington needed to take care of him. "Would you like for me to open that wine now?"

"Oh." Leo startled a little, as if he had already forgotten about the bottles he held. He held the white out to Remington. "You can open this one, if you'd like." He shook the red at them. "This one I opened in the driveway." He took a swig before holding it out to them, offering them a drink.

Roscoe accepted. He held Leo's stare as he sipped. Then he passed the bottle back. "You should finish it. That way, we know we have you for the night."

Leo immediately turned up the bottle, proving how nervous he was. Remington stole a moment to eye his body. He wore a sheer black blouse that molded to his skin and black pants that shaped his perfect ass and thighs. He was small and beautiful. Snack-sized. Roscoe ran his hand down Remington's back, pulling Remington from his thoughts. He didn't doubt he looked as intense as he felt. Leo had his hunger churning.

"Let's find some glasses."

Remington led the way. He headed for the bar in the corner of their living room. With one eye locked on Leo, he grabbed three wine glasses while Leo wandered over to their Christmas tree. He inspected the gold ornaments.

"Until I walked into the coffeehouse today and saw their tree, I hadn't realized how close we are to the holidays."

Roscoe moved to the leather couch and sat. "Do you have plans to go home to Texas to see your family?"

Leo tossed a sad smile their way. "No. There's no one back home but my dad now, and I have no desire to ever see him again. So it'll likely be my first Christmas alone. I noticed The Back Porch is open that day. Maybe I'll check out their vibe for the day."

Remington and Roscoe exchanged a glance. They would not let Leo be alone on Christmas. "You could hang out with us," Remington offered. "Our moms are in France this year, so we plan to have a quiet day at home. That probably doesn't sound exciting, but we always cook a bunch of food and watch movies all day."

Leo flashed a sweet smile. "Thanks for the offer, but I wouldn't want to intrude." His smile turned sad. "Plus, I can't imagine either of you will talk to me again after tonight."

Remington set their glasses on the coffee table and crossed the room to where Leo stood. Without a word, he snagged Leo's arm and led him to the couch. He took the wine from Leo before urging him to sit. Roscoe and Remington squished Leo between them on the couch. They didn't discuss it or exchange any glances. Roscoe simply grabbed a blanket and Remington grabbed the wine glasses. They reclined the sofa and cuddled Leo between them. A thought hit Remington as they settled in. Maybe tonight hadn't been about sex after all. It was possible they had sensed Leo needed a friend. Whatever the reason for Leo being there, Remington was grateful. They wouldn't let him be alone. He was too sweet for this ugly world. Roscoe and Remington could soothe him.

LEO DIDN'T KNOW WHAT to think. The night wasn't going the way he expected. With two bottles of wine consumed and a movie playing, he couldn't focus on anything except every touch beneath the blanket they shared. Leo expected one of the men to make a move any second. As the end credits rolled on their movie night, Leo wondered if he had misread the situation and now he couldn't drive home because of the wine. Truthfully, he felt a bit idiotic. They were so nice and obviously in love. He thought Remington and Roscoe had been pretty clear in their intentions. Hadn't they? He doubted his own mind.

Leo wondered if he should call a cab. It was getting late. His eyelids were getting heavy. It had been a long day.

Remington turned off the TV.

Roscoe folded the blanket.

The pair stood.

Remington held his hand out to Leo. "Bedtime."

Leo accepted without thinking. "Thanks for the movie. I'll call a cab and let y'all get some sleep."

The men smiled. It was simultaneous —like they shared one brain.

"That country accent jumped out for a second."

Roscoe nodded at Remington's observation. "That was hot. You don't need to call anyone. You're coming to bed with us."

Leo knew he looked like a blinking idiot. He had come here for this, but still he was unsure. "Okay." His mouth spoke, answering for the rest of him without his input.

Roscoe led the way, heading up the stairs. Remington stayed on Leo's heels. Leo's pulse pounded in his ears. The pair seemed so calm, as if they did this every day. Leo's throat swelled. Maybe they did do this every day. It was possible he was just another fun night to them. Leo's spine stiffened. That was fine. Life had been exhausting and harder than he expected for months now. He deserved this slice out of time. They were married. Leo didn't have to worry about anyone getting the wrong impression. He could just take what he wanted. No regrets. No looking back.

Roscoe peeled off his shirt.

Leo forgot everything he had ever known. He one thousand percent believed people paid to watch them. They probably made money hand over fist. Holy shit. Roscoe was abs and then some. Leo's mouth went dry. He stood in the middle of a massive yet sparsely decorated room, wondering what in the hell he had gotten into, when Remington's body molded against his back. Leo lost his breath.

Remington's lips touched Leo's ear. "You should get comfortable. Surely you can't sleep in these clothes."

Even though he didn't believe for a second they would be sleeping, Leo's hands immediately went to the button on his pants. Before he could get them unzipped, Roscoe quickly closed the distance between them and claimed Leo's mouth. His heart leapt into his throat as their tongues played. He wondered if he should feel guilty or awkward. None of that happened. Remington grasped Leo's jaw and turned Leo's head his way. His kiss was sweeter than Roscoe's, easing Leo even more. The pair tugged at Leo's clothes. Leo switched between kissing each man while his clothes disappeared. He felt like he was trapped in a whirlwind. Everything had gone from a zero to a hundred in an instant. Leo didn't want to stop. For months now, he had been tensed and barely holding himself together. Until Roscoe and Remington touched him, Leo hadn't realized how close he had been to falling apart. Being caught in their storm was like finally getting to scream at the top of his lungs in the rain. It felt like an uncontrollable storm, tearing everything away. He was free.

As quickly as it started, everything calmed. They were nude and the kisses and touches turned sweet. A hint of confusion set in. Leo didn't want to feel anything. This was one night. Leo didn't want to think about the couple beyond the faintest fond memory. Their touches felt too real— like they meant them. It fucked with Leo's mind. Leo wasn't the one-night stand type. But he would be after tonight. These men would never speak to him or think of him. His body and face would quickly fade from their memories. None of those truths stopped Leo. He wanted to lose himself.

The pair shuffled him toward the bed. He found himself on the mattress between them, urging them to kiss because he wanted to watch. They were so beautiful in their sexuality. It was oddly comforting, knowing they existed. Leo couldn't imagine being loved the way they loved each other. They accepted each other in a way Leo had never witnessed.

Then Roscoe kissed his way down Leo's body and Leo didn't think anymore. Roscoe had a porn star's mouth. It had Leo ready for anything. Remington straddled Leo's head and led his dick to Leo's mouth. Leo opened. He took everything the pair gave. His skin burned. Leo's mind twisted and turned with every new detail. His body writhed. Fingers massaged inside him, while Roscoe's throat tightened around his cock. Roscoe sucked and pumped, making Leo insane. Leo blew Remington in all the ways he wanted to be pleasured. Nothing mattered but the race toward release. Cum filled his mouth, nearly choking him as he cried out for more. Roscoe moaned around Leo's dick. The vibration of the sound sent Leo flying. He shook and twitched while

Roscoe sucked him dry. Leo floated on a cloud, losing himself to the moment. If anyone else knew the same euphoria as him, Leo couldn't say. All he understood in that moment was his soul had been shaken. He didn't know if he could stay away from the pair, but he would. They weren't his.

ROSCOE COULDN'T STOP TOUCHING the men every place he could reach. He knew he should let the other men sleep, but he rode the high of the night way too hard. Leo was still between them. He hadn't left. They weren't finished with him yet. That blowjob had only been a preview of what they had planned. Oddly, Roscoe wasn't in a hurry. He enjoyed this part too. Cuddling was some seriously underrated shit. He wanted more before demanding Leo's body in other ways.

"Why don't you want to go home for Christmas?"

Remington's whisper cut through the dark. Roscoe's curiosity spiked. He had wanted to ask that too, but he didn't want to seem like he was prying.

Leo didn't answer right away. When he finally spoke, his voice came out sounding hoarse. "Right before I left for L.A., my dad announced that after twenty-three years of marriage, he was leaving my mom for a girl at his work that he had been seeing behind my mom's back for two years. My mom had a stroke about a year ago and had been pretty weak ever since. The news devastated her. Her heart couldn't take the strain of learning he was cheating, and it just gave out. He's the reason she's dead and I can't live with that. So, now, he's every bit as dead to me."

Roscoe squeezed Leo as tightly as he could, as if he could squash the pain. His mom was the most amazing person he knew. It would kill him to lose her. He couldn't imagine what Leo was going through. Roscoe could tell the pain was still fresh. Roscoe could hear it in Leo's voice. His heart ached for Leo. He wanted to do something to fix it, but he knew there was nothing he could do.

Leo kissed the tip of Roscoe's nose, catching him off guard. Something tugged in his chest. There was just something incredibly sweet about the gesture. He liked it a little too much. He found Leo's mouth in the dark. The sensations in his chest turned to full-on pounding as their tongues brushed. He had been trying to be comforting. Instead, he felt too much.

Roscoe dragged Remington into their kiss. He needed to share this new passion with the man he loved more than life. He swore when Remington joined them, things clicked in a way he couldn't vocalize. He needed more.

Roscoe honestly didn't mean to go from learning Leo's mother had passed to having his fingers inside Leo's ass. Yet that was where he was. Remington, being the one who was always prepared, already had lube and condoms at the ready. Between kisses, Roscoe suited up and lubed Leo's asshole. He whispered words of praise as he shifted to his knees. Leo's tight hole gave way as Roscoe pushed his dick inside. He could barely breathe as Leo's body immediately tried sucking him deeper. Remington toyed with Roscoe's ass, splitting Roscoe's focus, and making him crazy. Then he found himself squashed between two bodies, as Remington took control and impaled his asshole.

Leo moaned beneath him.

Roscoe lost all ability to think while Remington set their pace. He held on and trusted the process. If Roscoe knew nothing else, he knew Remington would make him come. Roscoe sucked Leo's neck and focused on getting fucked. They were in for a long night. Roscoe was all in.

Chapter Three

WHILE SITTING ON THE countertop, Roscoe watched Remington cook. With nothing but boxer briefs molding his sexy round ass, Remington looked like a whole damn meal. Roscoe never stopped being bowled over by the amount of love he felt when he looked at his husband. Remington was the caretaker. He cooked, cleaned, and babied Roscoe. Back when they had first married, Remington had been the one who worked his fingers to the bone to keep a roof over their heads. It was also his genius at the exact right moment to fit the market to sell a stream of their sex life. They hit the internet at the perfect time to ride the wave on online porn popularity. They had made enough in their first two years to never work again if they chose. Then they had kept doing it. Lately, they were releasing content less and less often. Roscoe imagined they were almost done with sharing each other. That thought led to another: Leo.

The night kept running through Roscoe's mind. Leo was in the shower, getting ready for work, and Roscoe couldn't shake the feeling they needed to talk about him. They had shared a lot of men over the years. This one was different. They both knew it. Leo was special.

Remington turned away from the stove and caught Roscoe staring. A sexy and wicked smirk pulled at Remington's lips. "Were you checking out my ass?"

Roscoe didn't try to hide his infatuation. "Maybe."

"Good." Remington moved to stand between Roscoe's knees. "I'd hate to think you're bored with me."

Roscoe's heart twisted at the idea. His smile fell. "Don't say that to me."

A line appeared between Remington's eyebrows. "What's wrong, baby? You should know I'm joking."

Roscoe shook his head, hoping to shake off the weird moment. "Nothing's wrong. I just worry sometimes that you think... never mind. I don't know what I'm saying."

Remington held Roscoe's stare. He didn't look away. His eyes screamed with understanding. As always, it was like Remington read his mind. "I don't think this is about boredom. We've always both been all in. Otherwise, it wouldn't happen."

Despite his best efforts to wait until there was no chance of Leo walking into their conversation, Roscoe couldn't let the chance pass him by.

"What do you want for Christmas, by the way?" Remington asked before Roscoe found the words he needed.

"Leo."

A smile exploded across Remington's face at Roscoe's quick answer. "You really like him, huh?"

Roscoe nodded. He couldn't explain the instant attraction, but having Leo hadn't been enough. Roscoe wanted more.

Remington looked lost in thought. His eyes were unfocused, as if he saw only the images inside his head. Roscoe watched him with his heart in his throat. Finally, Remington focused on him again. "I've been trying to figure out a way to keep him, but—honestly —I can't fully read him."

"It's like he needs us, but then again, he doesn't," Roscoe said, getting into the conversation. It was possible Leo's overabundance of confidence, coupled with a visible independent streak, were the exact reasons they were so interested. But all that aside, there was something Leo kept hidden. There was a greediness to his kisses and touches, as if he feared each one would be his last.

Remington nodded. "Agreed. I don't want to break what's beautiful about him, but we need to convince him to stay somehow."

Roscoe couldn't stop smiling now that the truth was out there. They genuinely liked this one. He didn't know what they expected from Leo, but Roscoe knew they weren't through with him yet. They hadn't gotten to do all the things Roscoe wanted. Leo had to give them more time.

"Oh, my gosh. Something smells amazing."

Roscoe's gaze snapped to the kitchen doorway. Leo was the picture of innocence and beauty, even though he had proven there was nothing innocent about him last night.

"Remington made omelets. You'll love his cooking."

Leo glanced at his watch. "I have a shoot this morning, but I can definitely make time. If I'm quick, that is."

So many dirty images ran through Roscoe's mind. He could make Leo come fast while he ate. When he put his mind to it, Roscoe was very, very good.

Instead, Remington jumped in with both feet. He grabbed Leo a plate and filled it before passing it and a fork Leo's way. "We've been talking, and we want you to stay with us through the holidays. You shouldn't spend this first year without your mom alone and we like having you around."

Leo stood frozen, looking like a deer in headlights with a plate of food in his hands. "Oh. Um. Okay. I guess I could do that."

Remington looked Roscoe's way and winked. Then moved to fix their plates.

Leo took careful bites while standing in the center of the kitchen, as if he didn't know what to do with himself.

With a shake of his head, Roscoe hopped down from the counter and snagged Leo's waist. "Come on. Why do you look so nervous? There's zero reason to feel awkward about anything in this house. Sit. Eat." He pulled a stool out at the island and pointed at it.

Leo sat gingerly on the edge, as if ready to make a run for it. "Okay."

Roscoe moved to the fridge and grabbed a juice box from inside. When he sat it on the counter, in front of Leo's plate, Leo's eyes danced with laughter.

"A juice box. How old are you?"

"Three and a half years old," Remington quipped, beating Roscoe to the punch line.

Roscoe snorted. "Twenty-seven. How old are you?"

Leo stabbed the tiny straw into the top of the box. "Not too old for these, I guess. But seriously, twenty-one."

He looked adorable, drinking from the minuscule straw. Remington and Roscoe moved at the same time. Leo set his juice aside and pushed his plate away, as if he would rather have them. As they came together to hold one another, Roscoe was struck again by the eerie sensation of how well they fit —like they had been carved from the same soul. Everything felt right. They had to keep going.

THE STUDIO WHERE LEO worked was literally part of Dame's massive estate. In the poshest area of L.A., Leo steered his Lexus down the driveway and past the oversized mansion to a secondary home on the property. The second building was nearly as large as the first, except inside, it was one large, open area with sections for different photography sessions.

Once inside the red brick building, Leo rushed to the dressing room area. He wasn't late, but he wasn't as early as usual either and he still needed to get into wardrobe. If he didn't hurry, he would be late. Ezra was already waiting and flawless, as always. His light pink highlights were on point. Leo wanted to sigh at the first glance of him. Ezra was easily the most beautiful man Leo had ever seen. In fact, Ezra had once been voted the most beautiful man in the world. Leo felt like a frog in his presence. Thankfully, Ezra was also the nicest person Leo had ever met. As the brother of one of the biggest names in rock history, Leo would expect Ezra to be a spoiled bitch, but no. He was the epitome of kindness.

As Leo practically skidded into the dressing area, Ezra glanced his way. His hazel eyes widened. "Holy shot. What happened to you?" He rushed to Leo's side with foundation already at the ready. "We have to get these hickeys covered before Dame sees."

Leo winced. He hadn't even realized. "I went to The Back Porch yesterday, as you suggested, and met these guys."

Ezra nodded as he worked to cover the marks on Leo's skin. "Uh huh. Remington and Roscoe."

Leo froze. "How did you know that?"

Ezra kept his eyes locked on his task. "That's a ride everyone's been on, but continue."

For a moment, Leo wondered if he should be insulted or ashamed. Neither of those emotions rose to the surface, so Leo kept going. "Anyhow, I went to their place, and we watched a movie."

Ezra straightened away. His gaze locked on Leo's. He looked engrossed. "Really?"

Leo nodded. "Afterward, we obviously had some fun, but then we stayed up all night talking, and they're so, so kind. They invited me to stay with them through the holidays, so I won't be alone and missing my mom by myself. Remington made me breakfast and I'm just so fucking confused now. And... why are you looking at me like that?" Seriously, Ezra stared at Leo like he had grown a second head.

Ezra set the makeup aside, as if trying to compose himself. "I'm sorry. Did you say you spent the night at their place, and they invited you to stay for the next month?"

Leo's confusion grew. "Yeah. Why?"

Ezra shook his head slowly, as if working his way through some cobwebs. "Sweetie, I have been going to The Back Porch since I moved to L.A. a decade ago. I have watched those guys go home with every fresh face that walked through the door, but never—not one time—have they invited anyone to their place. In fact, everyone knows their place is off limits. The boys are up for a good time, but their bed is... well, their bed."

Leo could only blink in confusion. Ezra's claim didn't match his experience. "Huh. I didn't really get that impression." Leo peeled off his clothes while he spoke. "Not that it matters. I'm still not a hundred percent sold on the idea. I don't want to be a charity case, you know? I don't want to make a huge mistake here either."

A dark-haired assistant stuck his head in the door. "Fifteen seconds."

"Dang it. We need to get you dressed."

Leo bit back a smile. He had always found it humorous Ezra didn't curse. After all, words were just words, but Leo also got it. Ezra was so sweet. No one likely believed he was angry unless he brought out the big guns and dropped an F bomb. Leo stepped into a sleek black dress. His phone dinged as Leo zipped up the back.

"Goddamn it. Do you mind dealing with that so it's not dinging the whole shoot? You know my passcode," Leo called over his shoulder as he rushed from the room while simultaneously hopping into the black combat boots Dame had paired with the dress. He didn't wait for a response. No one ever texted Leo anything important. He wasn't worried Ezra would be burdened with anything pressing.

As usual, Dame wore a brightly colored wig—hot pink today—and matching lipstick. He flashed Leo a bright smile. "Gorgeous, as always. Now get your ass in gear. Time is money, darling."

Leo had been doing shoots with Dame for long enough he knew to switch between being as outrageous as possible and natural, so Dame would have lots of choices for his monthly catalog. He didn't hold back.

Ezra appeared behind Dame, holding Leo's phone. "The boys want to know if you want anything special from the grocery store."

Leo shook his head. "I know where the store is if I need anything."

Dame hiked the skirt above Leo's knees and took some more photos.

"Roscoe says he knows you know where the store is, but he wants you to be happy during your stay."

Dame turned Ezra's way. "Wait. You don't mean the Roscoe and Remington, do you?" He didn't wait for Ezra's confirmation before looking Leo's way. "You're staying with Roscoe and Remington?"

Subconscious didn't begin to cover Leo's feelings. "Yes."

Dame's long fake eyelashes batted several times. "At their house?"

Ezra flanked Dame and saved Leo from answering. "Yep. They've invited him to stay through the holidays."

Dame looked between them, mouth agape. "Shut the fuck up." Dame snapped his mouth closed and looked thoughtful. "Damn, boy, you must be fire in the sack."

Heat exploded through Leo's face.

Dame immediately started snapping pictures again. "Yes, King. Give me that innocent look. Men will eat you alive. Rawr."

Ezra chuckled. "I'll just tell the boys you'll text them after your shoot."

Leo nodded his thanks and went back to going through the paces. For the hundredth time, he wondered if he should be ashamed of being the obvious one millionth customer to Remington and Roscoe's bed. Then again, according to Ezra, he was the first. Maybe he wasn't making a mistake after all.

REMINGTON PLAYFULLY BUMPED ROSCOE with the shopping cart. He loved it when Roscoe shot annoyed looks his way. They hadn't put a single thing in the basket since they arrived ten minutes earlier. Roscoe was still waiting to hear what Leo wanted. Remington was bored and always spiraled into childishness when he had too much time on his hands.

"What's the holdup?" He tried bumping Roscoe with the cart again.

Roscoe sidestepped him at the last second. "I can't get an answer from Leo. I think he plans to ditch us."

Remington left the cart where they stood. "Fuck that. It's been a while since we've seen Dame. Let's crash his shoot. We can get groceries when we have Leo properly kidnapped."

A bright smile lit Roscoe's face. "Agreed. It has been way too long since we saw Dame."

They headed for their SUV without a qualm. In the past, they had done several nude photo shoots for Dame. They knew exactly where to go. Remington cut through a few subdivisions, easily avoiding traffic. They were headed down Dame's driveway in no time. Remington didn't doubt for a second that Leo planned to run for the hills. Leo wasn't like them. Roscoe and Remington were co-dependent as hell. Leo was obviously determined to not lean on anyone. They needed to teach him it was okay to let go of his independence occasionally. There was nothing wrong with needing someone else.

At Dame's studio, they jumped from the Tahoe and stormed into the building. They easily found Dame, Ezra, and Leo working at a green screen. Remington's steps faltered at the first sight of Leo. He wore a black dress that looked a bit punk and hugged his body. A pair of unlaced combat boots completed the outfit. He made Remington's mouth water. Every touch they shared invaded Remington's mind. He needed Leo to need them. There was no other option, as far as Remington was concerned.

Dame glanced behind him as they plopped down on a nearby loveseat to watch. "The two R's, as I live and breathe." Dame didn't ask why they were there. That made Remington happier than it should. That meant Leo wasn't ashamed. He had told people about them.

Roscoe flashed a naughty smile Dame's way. "Hello, Damey." He winked at Ezra. "Ez."

Remington gave Leo a heated once over before he focused on Ezra. He wore a dark tux with a full black shirt and vest. His makeup looked gorgeous. "Hey, beautiful. What are you up to?"

A devilish glint lit Ezra's eyes. He tossed a phone toward them. Roscoe caught it. "That's Leo's. Be careful. It's still unlocked. I'm here for this." He stepped in front of the camera with Leo and snagged Leo's waist. The pair went hip to hip, holding each other's stare. It was intense and sexy as hell.

Remington's skin heated even as his jealousy spiked. His instant reaction caught Remington off guard. The only person to ever stir his jealousy was Roscoe. No one touched his husband without his permission. It seemed he felt the same about Leo. Even though he knew Ezra and Leo were merely doing their job, Ezra had his hands all over Remington's man and Leo hadn't even greeted them yet. If he was happy to see them at all, Leo hadn't shown it.

Roscoe elbowed him, pulling his attention away from the pair in front of the camera. He glanced down at the device Roscoe held for him to see. Remington had been so lost in staring at Leo, it took him a second to realize what he looked at. It was texts on Leo's phone.

Dad: *You're an ungrateful bastard. Anastasia makes me happy. She deserves your respect. I fully expect you to be here on Christmas morning with bells on and your best manners on display.*

Leo: *No, thank you.*

Dad: *You'll be here. Wearing men's clothes like the man you were born to be and acting right, or you're as dead to me as your mother.*

Remington's throat swelled. He met Roscoe's stare. They didn't need to speak. This was something they understood too well. They had amazing moms who couldn't be replaced, but their fathers hated them for who they were. That was why their parents divorced and their moms lived together now. It was also why they hadn't spoken to their fathers in several years.

Roscoe leaned into Remington's side and held the phone out. He opened the camera, and they posed for a few pictures for Leo to keep on his phone. They would save Leo, even if he didn't realize he needed to be rescued.

Dame sighed loudly. "I can see your eyes begging me. Go greet your men and get back here."

As Remington looked on, a bright smile lit Leo's face. Remington realized Leo hadn't been ignoring them. He took his job seriously and didn't want to lose it. Dame snapped a few pictures of Leo's happiness before Leo got away. Leo quickly jogged to their side and kissed them. Remington knew his heart had to be in his eyes. He was thrilled to have Leo's attention.

Leo glanced between them. "I thought you two were shopping."

"We decided to wait until you go with us," Roscoe answered for them.

Remington nodded. "Maybe that way, you'll let us buy food you like."

Leo's eyes danced with happiness and laughter. "I'm perfectly capable of finding a store, if I'm hungry."

It was hard, but Remington fought a growl. "We're going together." He left no doubt it was an order.

Leo's smile didn't dampen. "Okay. I have to finish this shoot, but then I'm free until after the first of the year. Dame is headed to Italy, so no work for me."

"We'll take care of you."

Remington smiled at the way Roscoe and he said the words at the same time. It had always been like they shared one brain. He glanced Dame's way to test the man's impatience. He found Ezra and Dame watching them, wearing matching expressions of shock. Remington dismissed them to focus on Leo. He took Leo's hand. Their fingers linked. Leo bit his bottom lip, as if trying to hide his happiness, as Roscoe took his other hand.

"We'll wait for you to finish." Even Remington heard the innuendo in his voice.

Roscoe nodded. "We like to watch."

"Goddamn," Dame said, sounding breathless. "I miss being young."

A smile exploded across Remington's face. The heat between them had nothing to do with age. Remington wasn't sure it even had anything to do with sex. There was something in

Remington's chest, pulling him toward Leo. He had to explore it. They couldn't stop.

THE GUYS STAYED THROUGH Leo's shoot. They were a huge distraction and made things take way longer than necessary, but Dame was obviously too charmed by them to mind. In fact, no one seemed immune to their charms. Even Dame's assistant kept trying to fetch them drinks and doted upon them. Leo could only shake his head. He didn't know why the couple had crashed their way into his life, but here they were. Leo was more grateful than he could express. That was exactly why he had to shield his heart. They were married. Leo was just a distraction. In the end, they would leave him in the dust. The way everyone did.

Leo chewed his bottom lip as he drove to his apartment, with the guys following closely behind. It was obvious they had no intention of allowing Leo a chance to slip from their grasp. They planned to help Leo pack for his stay, leaving him with no chance to change his mind. He would stay with them for the next month or so. Leo had to take several deep breaths at the thought.

Last night had been amazing. He hadn't stopped smiling today. And all of that was the issue. Since his mom's passing, he had learned some really hard lessons. The biggest one was that he was completely alone in the world. There was no one coming to save him. Something inside Leo had hardened since he moved to L.A. If he failed or broke in any way, there was no soft place for him to land. He would be homeless if he wavered. Leo got the impression Remington and Roscoe had never known a life like his. They had always had each other. Even though he liked them a lot, they weren't the same as him. They couldn't understand him.

As he parked outside his apartment and stepped from his car, Leo's heart tried doing a cartwheel in his chest as the men climbed from their SUV. They were so exquisite. Despite all his reservations, Leo wasn't backing down. No matter what happened, he knew he wouldn't regret the time they gave him.

Remington rubbed his hands together. "We know where you live now. You're in our grasp." He released a maniacal laugh, like a cartoon villain.

Leo rolled his eyes, but deep down, he smiled. He wanted to be in their grasp. "The place isn't much. Obviously, it's nowhere near as nice as your place, but it is what it is."

Roscoe snorted. "When we moved into our first place, it was like someone had cleaned out a closet and rented the place. We didn't even have a stove."

Remington nodded along. "All we had was a microwave and a mini fridge." He shrugged. "But we made do. It's just a roof and walls."

It really wasn't. Not to Leo. He had nowhere else to go, but he couldn't say that. Plus, he appreciated they were trying to set him at ease. Leo led them inside. The place was a bit of a mess. He hadn't intended to have visitors... ever. It wasn't the soiled kind of unclean, but there were discarded clothes sitting around that he hadn't felt like folding or hanging... or ironing.

"Sorry, it's a mess. I've been busy with Dame, trying to get his latest catalog completed before he leaves town. Life has been a bit hectic." Leo didn't look their way as he picked up clothes and headed for the bedroom. He needed to drag out his luggage if he planned to pack enough clothes to stay with them until after the first of the year. Leo froze. That was more than a month away. Actually, it was nearly five weeks. It was possible this was a terrible idea. They didn't know him. Not really. He didn't know them either. The closer he got to going to stay with them, the more insane things sounded. Surely people didn't stay with people after a one-night stand like this. Maybe this was a mistake.

Remington's body molded against Leo's back, and Leo knew it was him without looking. That thawed his brain. Then Roscoe moved to stand toe to toe with Leo, and everything felt right. He remembered exactly why this hadn't felt like insanity this morning. There was something here between the three of them. It grew bigger by the second.

Leo's thoughts voiced themselves before he realized it would happen. "What is happening with us? Why do I feel like this?"

Roscoe's expression softened. His gaze moved over Leo's face. "You tell us. We've never come back for seconds or invited anyone to our place. What is it about you? Why can't we stay away?"

It was oddly comforting to know he wasn't the only one who didn't understand this draw between them.

Remington's lips brushed Leo's shoulder. "We didn't even have to talk about it. From the moment we saw you, we knew you were special." His lips moved to Leo's neck. "So stop thinking."

Roscoe pushed aside the clothes Leo held and invaded his space. "You're safe with us."

Something inside Leo gave way. He had been barely holding himself together for too long.

Remington kissed his ear. "It's time to pack your things."

It was. Leo had to stay with them.

Chapter Four

AFTER SPENDING THE DAY running errands, getting Leo settled, and then having dinner together, they tossed a blanket on the floor in front of a fake crackling fire in their fireplace and cuddled. Unexpected smiles kept touching Roscoe's lips. His happiness level was almost frightening. He worried he had been given too much. Surely everything would come crashing down soon. Every caress felt like a dream. He wanted to bask in the glow forever.

"How did you two end up together?" The whispered question cut into Roscoe's thoughts. Leo didn't stop there. "I mean, like I know you two grew up best friends and glued at the hip, but I want to hear the story of you confessing your feelings and all that."

Remington laughed, and Roscoe bit back a groan. He knew Remington was about to tell every sordid detail.

"Well," Remington said, proving Roscoe wasn't wrong. "I had always assumed we were together—like together, together—and that Roscoe understood he was mine. But then, when we were fifteen, he told me a guy at school had kissed him in the bathroom and they had a date planned for the upcoming Saturday night."

Leo moved up onto his elbow so he could hold Remington's stare. He looked scandalized. "No."

Remington nodded, being every bit as dramatic as he had been when it happened years ago. "Yep. I was pissed."

"I'll bet."

Roscoe rolled his eyes at the pair. "It wasn't even a good kiss, and I was only trying to make Remington jealous. He claims I should've known I was his, but he never gave me a reason to know it. I don't think he had even held my hand at this point."

Remington gasped, being outrageously fake. "I told you I loved you all the time."

Roscoe rolled his eyes and crossed his arms over his chest. "Go on and finish the story. You may as well tell it all."

A wicked smile stretched Remington's lips, and love filled Roscoe's chest. Remington was an obnoxious ass sometimes, but he was Roscoe's obnoxious ass. Remington didn't let him down. "So, Saturday night rolled around. I waited until he was getting ready to leave and I locked him in the bathroom."

Leo laughed.

Roscoe softened.

Remington kept going. "I sat on the floor outside the door, barricading it so he couldn't burst out."

"I could've gone out the window."

They ignored him. "I told him he wasn't going anywhere unless I went too, and he wasn't getting out of the bathroom until he admitted he was mine."

"And I had to apologize for being a cheat," Roscoe added.

Remington nodded. "And he had to apologize for being a *dirty* cheat."

Leo looked invested. "How long did it take for you to do all that?"

Smiles exploded across Roscoe's and Remington's faces. Roscoe jumped in first to tell the rest. "I didn't. Instead, I talked dirty to him through the door until I lured him into the bathroom with me. Then when he started kissing me, I slipped out and locked him inside."

A surprised-sounding bark of laughter burst from Leo. He covered his mouth to hide the sound, but his eyes swam with laughter. He dropped his hand and his voice to a whisper. "Please tell me you didn't go on your date."

Roscoe shook his head. His throat swelled at the memory. "I told him I loved him through the door and asked him to marry me. From that moment on, it was understood that it would always be only us and we would not be pursuing anyone else separately."

A sweet smile touched Leo's lips as he settled down beside them again. Roscoe drew a ragged breath. He loved being between them. Leo's hand slid across Roscoe's stomach. Roscoe closed his eyes and savored the sensation. Remington kissed his forehead. The truth hit Roscoe so hard, he nearly shot from the floor. He was a sponge and Remington was a running faucet. Roscoe soaked up love and always wanted more while Remington had too much to give and needed a place for his love to go. And —with all his heart—Roscoe believed Leo was an empty well, waiting for them to fill him. Everything had been emptied from Leo's life and now he needed exactly what Remington and Roscoe offered: an overabundance of neediness and love. They could fill him and consume him. He was the perfect fit for them.

REMINGTON COULDN'T STOP STARING at the men beside him. With his elbow on the floor and his head braced on his palm, he eyed the pair. They were different in so many ways, but also the same. He wondered what he had done so right to deserve them. Remington was a caretaker to his core. Seeing those texts from Leo's dad kept making his blood boil. When he had stepped inside Leo's apartment earlier, Remington had fought the urge to start packing boxes. Roscoe and he had a home and hearts that could easily take Leo in and love him the way he deserved. Between those texts and telling that story about Roscoe nearly slipping away from him, Remington felt possessive as hell tonight.

"We should take a shower and get ready for bed." Even Remington heard the hunger in his voice.

"In a minute." Roscoe sounded every bit as hungry. "First, I want to watch."

Remington immediately went hard. There was no slow build. He knew that tone. Remington would be putting on a show for his husband.

Leo moved up onto his elbow. "You should be more specific." His hand moved to the button on Roscoe's jeans. "What exactly would you like to see?" As he posed the question, Leo's gaze met Remington's.

Remington's mouth went dry.

Roscoe didn't disappoint. "I want to watch your sexy lips close around my cock while Remington fucks you."

A pant burst from Remington. He wanted that too.

Leo moved to his knees. "I like this plan."

Remington rolled and pushed to his feet. "I'll grab condoms and lube." Remington's pulse pounded in his ears as he headed for the bedroom. Roscoe and he had always been overly sexual. They never held back. This felt different, though. They weren't simply taking their pleasure. He thought they might be staking a claim.

By the time he returned to the living room, Leo and Roscoe were already nude. Leo was on his knees, ass up and choking on dick. Remington's cock twitched hard. He couldn't get undressed quick enough. Leo's round ass called to be invaded. Remington rolled a condom down his length and squirted lube everywhere. He didn't try to be careful. The scene playing out in front of him was too hot. He tried to be somewhat patient and stretch Leo's hole before pushing his crown inside.

A loud moan sounded around Roscoe's cock. Roscoe writhed. Remington watched the entire show with zero patience left. He needed more. Remington shoved forward, impaling Leo. Roscoe watched with lust glimmering in his eyes. Leo sounded like he loved every second. Remington held Leo's hips and pumped. His gaze moved between watching his dick saw in and out of Leo's ass to watching the way Roscoe savored every second. Leo's muffled moans got louder. He reached between his legs and jacked off while sucking Roscoe's dick and taking everything Remington gave. Everything sped and slowed. He wanted this to last all night. Fuck. He wanted this to last forever.

Realization struck Remington like getting hit by a truck. He could do this for the rest of his life. Remington could take care of two men. Leo matched them perfectly, and it felt like he belonged with them. They could make this work.

Roscoe cried out.

Remington's focus snapped to him. He watched as Roscoe came unglued, filling Leo's mouth with cum. Then Leo's body unexpectedly tried sucking him deeper as Leo shot his load on the blanket covering the living room floor beneath them. Remington lost his ability to do anything but feel. He pumped faster and harder, racing toward the edge. When the pressure turned to pleasure, Remington swore he saw stars.

As he collapsed beside his men, his gaze met Roscoe's. A silent understanding passed between them. This had been meant to be. He knew then he would do anything to keep the three of them together. Leo was part of them now. They were officially a throuple.

Chapter Five

EACH DAY THAT PASSED with Remington and Roscoe, Leo got a little more attached. They were like giant kids, and it was catching. A month under their roof felt like forever. Not getting attached wasn't an option any longer. On Christmas Eve, they left Leo alone while they went shopping for Leo's presents. He stole the chance to shop for them as well. While he didn't have a ton of money to spend, he tried to make things special. He knew Roscoe liked putting together model cars and Remington enjoyed gaming. He ran with that and bought what he could.

When they got home, the guys dragged Leo back out to several stores and forced him to pick out an ornament for the tree. He didn't think it was that big of a deal until he stared at a long row of ornaments and watched the guys debate which one best fit Leo's personality and which one best represented their time together. Then Leo realized how important this yearly tradition was to them, and he was being included. When Leo spotted the perfect ornament, it felt like a sign. It was a tiny Christmas tree with three boys signing carols around it. Two of the boys were dark-haired, and the other was blond. It was them. Leo felt it. They had immediately taken home their find and then split into separate rooms to wrap their presents. For the first time since Leo was a kid, he felt like he had a steady home.

That thought was enough to punch Leo in the chest with reality. His throat hurt. Remington and Roscoe weren't his. They had a life and a marriage. He didn't know why they had decided to include him in their family festivities this year. But this wasn't his life or his home, and soon he would have to go back to being alone. He needed to accept that. The knowledge was enough to break him. His phone dinged while he sat surrounded by ribbon and wrapped gifts. It took him a minute of digging through scraps of wrapping paper to find it. When he spotted his dad's number, Leo's heart dropped. He reluctantly opened his messages.

Dad: *I gather by your absence you have no intention of coming home this year. I guess it's for the best. Anastasia and her family have never approved of your lifestyle choices, and I know you wouldn't have resisted the chance to embarrass me. She's been telling me for a while now that we should make this separation between us permanent. I think she's right. You'll never change and every day I keep reaching out for you is a day I get farther from God. I just wanted to let you know I'm blocking your number. Don't bother calling anymore.*

The phone slipped from Leo's fingers. Everything hurt. He had known for a while they would never speak again. His heart obviously hadn't completely accepted it. A tear dropped onto his wrist. Leo didn't have what it took to wipe his face. It was harder than expected, being completely alone. He wanted to be an island, but he felt like a rapidly sinking ship.

"Hey, I'm not looking, but we're making..." Roscoe's words died as he peeked inside the room. He gave up any pretense of giving Leo privacy and stepped inside. "What's going on?"

Leo swiped at his cheeks as he unlocked his phone and passed it Roscoe's way. It didn't matter who knew. His life was what it was.

Remington appeared in the doorway while Roscoe's gaze moved over the message. "Why is everyone hiding in here?"

Roscoe held the phone out to Remington. As soon as Remington relieved him of the device, Roscoe pulled Leo into his arms and held him.

"It doesn't matter." Even Leo heard the lie in his voice.

Remington joined them on the floor and held them both. He kissed their foreheads and some of the pressure lifted from Leo's chest. Maybe they weren't his, but—for now—they were here. Leo needed them.

A solid ten minutes passed while Remington held them before Remington finally broke the silence. "We didn't finish the story about us admitting our love. Roscoe finally stopped barricading the bathroom door and slipped inside with me. His dad came looking to see what all our antics had been about, and he caught us in an extremely compromising position." Leo's attention was caught. He realized he hadn't heard the guys talk about their fathers. Only their moms. He hung on every word. "Roscoe's dad called my dad and a huge fight erupted between everyone while we watched in horror. Our dads blamed our moms for shoving us together all our lives. Threats were made about never letting us see each other again."

Leo leaned away. Horror raced through him. Obviously, things had worked out, but he couldn't even fathom the thought of them being separated. "Oh my god. What happened?"

Roscoe flashed him a sad smile and picked up where Remington left off. "While the adults were still screaming at each other, we slipped from the room and ran. We lived for three weeks on the streets before Remington's mom found us and convinced us to come home. But honestly, those three weeks solidified us. We were more determined than ever not to break."

Leo could imagine. They were two people who should never be apart.

Remington shook his head. "Turns out, it was our parents that broke. While we had been living on the streets, my mom left my dad. Roscoe's dad left his mom. Our moms moved into my parents' house. So much had changed that our lives were nearly unrecognizable by the time we went home."

"We were suddenly living under the same roof," Roscoe chimed in. "But we had wrecked our parents. Neither of our dads speak to us anymore."

Remington nodded, finishing for Roscoe. "Our moms still live together. They're really living their best lives now, but we endured a lot before our dads stopped speaking to us. They called us names and tried to force us into conversion therapy. It was ugly. But just like us, you're not alone."

A sad smile pulled at the corners of Leo's mouth. "You have each other. I have nothing but an empty apartment and a job that'll last as long as Dame's interest does. We are not the same."

Roscoe and Remington exchanged a glance.

Remington stood. "I'll be right back."

Before Leo had time to question his leaving, Remington was back. He reclaimed his spot on the floor. "We were planning to give this to you tomorrow, but I don't think it can wait." Remington handed Leo a small and brightly wrapped gift box. The pair stared at him expectantly.

"You want me to open this now?"

They nodded.

Leo unwrapped the gift and opened the lid. It was a key. His chin lifted along with his eyebrows. "What's this?"

Roscoe answered for them. "We want you to move in with us."

Although Leo's mouth didn't literally fall open, it was a narrow miss. "I'm sorry. What?"

The pair looked hopeful. Remington practically bounced in place. "You know, move in. Like we put your things in boxes and move them here. You sleep with us every night and we get to tell everyone you're ours."

Leo blinked. He had not seen this coming. "But why?"

They visibly lost a bit of their happiness. Roscoe looked a little less hopeful. "We care about you and want you in our lives."

"You just met me." Leo didn't know why he kept arguing. He wanted what they offered, but he was more than a little gun shy after his own dad had just dumped him. These amazing men who already had each other had no real reason to keep him.

Remington and Roscoe leaned closer to each other, as if bracing against his inevitable rejection. "Do you not care about us?"

At Remington's question, Leo's throat swelled. "It's not that. I'm just scared to hope, I guess. It's not like I planned to meet you. Now you're saying you care about me and want me while no one cares about me or wants to keep me. Where am I supposed to go with that?" He didn't want to get tossed aside again. Leo didn't want to lose them, and it didn't make sense. He had just met them. Leo shouldn't be this attached. His inner panic had him on the edge of hyperventilating.

Roscoe took his hand. "Take a breath and be honest with yourself. Are you happy here with us?"

Leo nodded.

The men wore matching sweet smiles. Remington grabbed the box from Leo and set it aside so he could pull Leo between them. "Listen, if you're happy and you care about us too, then stay. I know you weren't expecting us, but does that matter? You're wanted here. In fact, it's been breaking our hearts, thinking about you leaving at the first of the year. Let this be the family you choose. I swear we'll never stop choosing you back."

Leo was scared to hope, but that wasn't all he felt in the face of their earnestness. "I want this." His admission came out in a whisper, but it came from the depths of Leo's soul. He wanted this. He wanted them. Leo wouldn't lose his chance. This was real.

EVEN THOUGH LEO'S AGREEMENT had been the faintest whisper, Remington heard the desire behind Leo's words. Leo genuinely wanted to share his life with them too. There had been a tiny part of his heart that had been holding back. Remington honestly hadn't thought Leo would take them as they were. His throat swelled. He needed Leo to understand exactly how he made them feel by accepting them as they were.

"The day we met at the coffeehouse. You didn't look around while speaking to us, as if embarrassed and ensuring no one saw you with us. That's why we couldn't stay away."

Leo leaned away so he could see their faces. He looked fierce. "Why would I be embarrassed?"

Remington fell a little harder in that moment.

Roscoe answered, proving how their minds were always in sync. "Because we're those guys. We're the ones people come to when they want to lose themselves, but only if no one knows they came to us. We're the ones you don't let anyone see you with in public. Otherwise, people will whisper about you. It doesn't matter that we haven't gone home with anyone else in over a year or that no one has ever been in our bed, except for you. Even though we always make sure no one sits alone at The Back Porch, we're the outcasts."

A myriad of emotions crossed Leo's features. He looked surprised, then confused, and finally... outraged. "When you sat down with me, I was so relieved to not be alone, I hadn't been sure if I could really eat the cake Wrecker gave me. Since I came to town, I've been alone and self-conscious everywhere I go. It's like my shoulders never get to rest. I feel like people are staring and judging. When you sat with me, my shoulders relaxed for the first time in months. I ate without thinking. Everyone else disappeared. I could never be ashamed of being with the two of you. You're my best friends."

Remington's heart soared. "We feel the same and then some."

Roscoe leaned into Remington. Remington swore he could feel Roscoe's emotions. They were on the same page. Leo had stolen part of them, but he had given his whole self in return. It was humbling and beautiful. He couldn't wait to spend his life with them.

Leo swiped at his face and squared his shoulders. "I say we go to The Back Porch and get pie."

A laugh burst from Remington. "Right now?"

Roscoe happy-clapped. "Yes. I agree. Pie."

Leo gave them a sharp nod. "I just got dumped by my dad and it feels like we should celebrate. Let's go make people talk."

Remington couldn't stop smiling as he pushed to his feet. He had different thoughts about the way they should celebrate, but he was on board. Maybe it was time to get people talking again. After all, there was no time like the present for people to understand Leo belonged to them. He was off the market now, and so were they. They were done hunting. They had found their unicorn.

ROSCOE FELT LIKE HE walked on air as they stepped inside The Back Porch. It might have been Christmas Eve, but The Back Porch was always doubly packed on holidays. The coffeehouse that catered to mostly gay men was a haven for people whose families had turned their backs on them. So the place stayed open three hundred and sixty-five days a year to ensure everyone had a place to go where they wouldn't be alone.

Heads turned their way as they headed for an empty table. Roscoe took the inside chair. Leo sat beside him. Remington grabbed a chair, and they squeezed in as tightly as they could on one side of the table. Remington draped his arm across the backs of their chairs. Leo held Roscoe's hand beneath the table. Roscoe stared at a menu on the table to hide the smile he couldn't squelch.

Remington kissed Leo's cheek before looking past him to focus on Roscoe. "Does Wrecker have any of that chocolate pecan pie that he usually makes this time of year?"

Roscoe forced himself to focus on the paper holiday menu that had been taped to the table. "Yeah. It looks like it."

Leo leaned his way to look. "Oh. Really. That sounds delicious."

Remington caressed the back of Roscoe's neck. "If that's good with everyone. I'll order for us."

Roscoe and Leo nodded.

Wrecker appeared at the edge of their table. "Hey, guys. What can I get you?"

While Remington ordered, Roscoe pressed his lips to the shell of Leo's ear. "When we get home, I want to kiss you with Remington's cock between us."

Leo quickly turned his head and captured Roscoe's lips. He lingered. Roscoe's breath caught. He always felt more than he expected when they kissed. There was something between them that grew bigger every day.

When Leo pulled away, he turned Remington's way and whispered in his ear. Roscoe knew Leo passed the word along about their plans by the hungry way Remington stared at them.

"My babies," Remington said, sounding fierce, making Roscoe's muscles tense in anticipation.

Roscoe was in love with the life they shared. He was in love with these men. His thoughts had him holding his breath and searching his heart. They hadn't known Leo that long. But Leo had been with them every second for a month now, and every day, his feelings deepened. Not only was he completely certain Leo belonged with them and only them, but he was also in love with Leo. At the realization, he brought Leo's hand to his mouth and held it there. He placed several kisses on his knuckles.

"Hey. How are you three?"

Roscoe forced his attention away from Leo as a new shadow fell over their table. Ezra pulled out a chair across from them and sat. His gigantic husband, Declan, joined him.

Remington answered for them. "We're doing great. I thought your family celebrated Christmas on Christmas Eve."

Ezra nodded. "We do, but we also couldn't resist getting Wrecker's famous chocolate pecan pie."

Ezra's brother, Jessie, and Jessie's husband, Theo, came through the door. Even though Jessie was a rock god, everyone at The Back Porch was used to seeing him and left him in peace. He still looked punk as hell, even though he was retired. Jessie's gaze scanned the room and landed on them. A bright smile lit his face. He dragged his adorable husband their way.

"Hey, let's grab some chairs. Surely we can all squeeze in. I haven't seen you guys in a minute." His blue gaze landed on Leo. "You, I've never seen."

Leo held Jessie's gaze with a confidence only he could carry. "I'm Leo."

A bright smile lit Jessie's face. He hauled his husband forward. "Hey, Leo. This is Theo and I'm Jessie."

The way Leo smiled had Roscoe captivated. "It's nice to meet you both."

Their tiny and crowded table quickly became the loudest in the building. Pie and coffee arrived. More people stopped by to chat. By the time their plates were emptied and cleared away, everyone had met Leo and understood he belonged to Remington and Roscoe now. No one questioned them, but they got a ton of surprised yet envious stares. Roscoe got it. He was a lucky man. His cup definitely ran over with blessings.

The crowd thinned, and checks were paid. The brittle edge to Leo's features, left behind by his dad's text, had finally melted away. Remington shuffled them toward the SUV. He looked more than ready to have them to himself.

Roscoe lightly elbowed Leo and nodded Remington's way. Leo winked. They piled into the vehicle. Leo climbed into the backseat and waited until Remington got behind the wheel before he attacked. He snagged Remington's hair, pulled his head back, and captured his lips. While Leo kept Remington's mouth occupied, Roscoe went straight for the goods. He unbuttoned and unzipped Remington's pants and went down on him. He savored the way Remington's dick went from soft to hard on his tongue. Loud pants filled the SUV.

Leo talked dirty to Remington while Roscoe pleasured him. "Fuck his mouth, sexy. I want to watch. Show me how fast you can come. I want to see if you can pump Roscoe's throat full of cum before anyone sees."

Remington made a desperate sound that nearly had Roscoe coming in his jeans. Roscoe knew Remington's body. He knew how to make him suffer or he could make him blow faster than lightning. Remington fucked his mouth, taking what he wanted while Leo praised him. In no time, cries cut through the air and hot cum coated his tongue. Roscoe licked his lips as he pulled away. Remington grabbed his hair and hauled him in for a kiss. Leo tried moving back to the backseat. Remington wasn't having it. He snagged Leo before he could get away.

Remington sounded breathless and ragged as he spoke. His gaze moved between them. "I love you two. I never want to lose either of you. But when we get home, I plan to fuck you both like I hate you."

To Roscoe's surprise, tears filled Leo's eyes. "You love me?" His voice sounded hoarse and tiny, breaking Roscoe's heart.

Roscoe couldn't let Leo flounder. "We both do. You're ours now. But Remington is right, nothing sweet is happening tonight."

A blinding smile exploded across Leo's face. "That's fine. I love y'all too and nothing sweet is filling this ache I have in my soul for you both. Bring your worst."

Roscoe stared at the men who meant everything to him, and life made more sense than it ever had. This was what they had been searching for since the day they married. This was their family. They were whole and beautiful, and they needed to get home. Roscoe was about to fuck his name into their souls. This was forever.

Chapter Six

LEO WOULD BE LYING if he claimed his body didn't hurt everywhere and in the most delicious ways. His babies were still sleeping, but it was Christmas morning and Leo was wide awake. He slipped from the bed and padded to the kitchen. Leo eyed the contents of the refrigerator while he waited for the coffeemaker to do its thing.

Arms encircled his waist and dragged him backward. He knew without looking it was Roscoe. Roscoe kissed his nape and Leo's head fell forward, giving Roscoe better access. Roscoe slowly turned Leo in his arms. In no time, Leo's back was against the counter, and his tongue played with Roscoe's. They both wore only thin workout shorts and their bodies molded in every way. Leo couldn't stop touching Roscoe every place he could reach.

Roscoe pulled away, only far enough to touch his forehead to Leo's. "Merry Christmas."

"Merry Christmas, angels," Remington said from the doorway, pulling their focus his way. He had his phone held up, taking pictures. "We have to document this day. It's our first Christmas together."

Leo chuckled. "Are you taking pictures or a video to post online?"

Remington's expression turned wicked. "Now that's an excellent idea." He clicked around on his phone and then spoke toward the device. "Merry Christmas, everyone." He pushed his way between Roscoe and Leo while holding the phone out to get all three of their faces in frame. Leo was a bit apprehensive since he looked a hot mess, but he was too happy to jump out of view. Remington kissed both their cheeks before going back to talking to the camera. "We just woke up, so please excuse our appearance, but we thought this would be a great time to introduce you to Leo. Say hi, Leo."

Leo waved. He wondered if he should be upset by being ambushed like this, but he was too overjoyed to balk, and the guys looked too proud.

Roscoe jumped in. "While we haven't discussed Leo being in any of our online content, he's our heart and we wanted to be here as a family for the holidays. So, from our family to yours, happy holidays."

Remington killed the camera. "If no one has any objections; I'm uploading this now."

Leo glanced between them.

No one balked and he couldn't.

Remington clicked around on his phone, then set the device aside. "Who wants presents?"

Roscoe raced to the living room like a kid. Remington kissed Leo before he followed. Leo trailed behind, reeling. He watched his men sit on the floor beside the tree, and his heart skipped a beat. His throat swelled. He hadn't known a person could be so happy. It seemed like a year had passed since he had walked into The Back Porch, determined to keep his spine straight and head high. Now everything had changed.

Leo joined Roscoe and Remington on the floor. Remington passed out their gifts. Presents, love, and happiness surrounded Leo. He said a quick and silent prayer, thanking his mom for loving him from heaven. Leo knew without a doubt she had sent these men to him. There were blessings and then there were Christmas-time miracles. Remington and Roscoe were definitely that last one. He didn't doubt for a second this was forever, and Leo couldn't wait to spend the rest of his life with them. Life was perfect.

Please keep an eye out this January for the prequel to Candied Crush, *Beautifully Damaged.*

Please consider leaving a review at the retailer where you purchased this book. Reviews really help with a book's visibility, which allows me to continue writing more stories. Thank you, Charity.

About the Author

CHARITY PARKERSON IS AN award-winning and multi-published author with several companies. Born with no filter from her brain to her mouth, she decided to take this odd quirk and insert it in her characters.

*Eight-time Readers' Favorite Award Winner

*2015 Passionate Plume Award Finalist

*2013 Reviewers' Choice Award Winner

*2012 ARRA Finalist for Favorite Paranormal Romance

*Five-time winner of The Mistress of the DarkpathConnect with her online:

*Sign up for her newsletter: https://sendfox.com/charityparkerson

*Join her readers' group on Facebook: http://bit.ly/CharitysTribe

*Website: https://www.charityparkerson.com

*A list of her social media accounts and giveaways all in one place: http://hy.page/charityparkerson